GRANDPA'S FOLKTALES

by Dixie Marshall
illustrated by Alexandra Colombo

Harcourt

SCHOOL PUBLISHERS

Printed in China

ISBN 10: 0-15-351534-1
ISBN 13: 978-0-15-351534-7

Ordering Options
ISBN 10: 0-15-351214-8 (Grade 4 Advanced Collection)
ISBN 13: 978-0-15-351214-8 (Grade 4 Advanced Collection)
ISBN 10: 0-15-358124-7 (package of 5)
ISBN 13: 978-0-15-358124-3 (package of 5)

4 5 6 7 8 9 10 0940 12 11 10 09

One weekend, Kira and Jamal went to the
mountains to visit their grandparents. It was a hot
summer day, and the children were glad to be getting
away from the heat of the city. At the train station,
Grandpa gave Kira and Jamal a great big hug.
"Grandma is making a special dinner for us tonight,"
he said. With that, the three of them jumped into
Grandpa's old pickup truck and were off.

Beaver River was about one hundred miles from
the city, but not many people knew where it was or
how to get there. As Grandpa drove through the old
mountain pass, he noticed that some dark clouds had
gathered overhead. "Looks like some rain might come
our way," he observed. "We can always find something
to do indoors if we need to."

As the truck turned down Old River Road,
Grandma Jackson was already waiting anxiously
at the door. She didn't like the way the storm clouds
were moving in. As soon as she saw the old truck,
she breathed a little sigh of relief.

"Grandma, we hear you're making us some of your
special gumbo!" shouted Jamal.

"Someday, will you tell me your secret recipe?"
asked Kira.

"Well," Grandma declared, "perhaps I'll let the cat
out of the bag and tell you." At that moment, a great
clap of thunder roared overhead. The sky opened up,
and it began to pour.

"Quick, let's go inside!" shouted Grandpa.

All that day, the rain poured over the mountains.
Bolts of lightning flashed and thunder cracked.

As soon as everyone had finished dinner, the lights began to flicker. Then they flickered again and went out. Grandpa jumped up and turned on the radio. Electricity lines were down all over, and it seemed that the power would be out for quite some time.

Jamal and Kira looked at each other, distressed. What would they do without television, the computer, or the DVD player? "Well, now," said Grandpa, "when I was little, we would sit on the porch and tell tales. It's a tradition that came from my great-grandpa when he lived in Africa."

Jamal groaned and rolled his eyes at Kira just a little as if to say, "Oh, no, not Grandpa's stories again."

"Did I ever tell you the story about how the ostrich got its long neck?" smiled Grandpa as he sat back and began his story.

"A very long time ago, ostriches had short necks. It was difficult for the ostrich to eat because he could neither reach the berries on the trees nor the bugs on the ground. The ostrich had to sit on his very long legs to reach the ground.

"One day, the ostrich happened along a riverbank where a crocodile was napping. The crocodile opened one eye because it was getting close to dinnertime. You see, the crocodile was a rather clever fellow, and he figured that he would trick the ostrich.

" 'Oh, Ostrich,' said the crocodile. 'I have a terrible toothache. Could you put your head inside my mouth and take a look? You could pull out the bad tooth with your beak.' The crocodile opened up his jaws very wide.

"Well, now, the ostrich, not being a very bright fellow, stuck his head in the crocodile's mouth! The crocodile, thinking he had his dinner prepared and ready to go, closed his jaws on the ostrich's neck. The ostrich was not about to become dinner for the crocodile, so he began to pull. He pulled and pulled, but the crocodile pulled back, and soon, the ostrich's neck began to stretch. At last, the crocodile got tired, so he let go of the ostrich, and that is how the ostrich got its long neck," finished Grandpa.

"Where did these stories come from?" asked Jamal. "Who would invent such a silly story about an ostrich?"

"Well," Grandpa explained, "many years ago, people in Africa did not have televisions or radio or electricity. They made up stories to pass the time and to amuse themselves. Tribes would often gather around a fire, and people would tell stories. The stories were meant to explain why things were a certain way, or things that people didn't understand. Over many years, these folktales were passed down through family members. I remember many of these stories because my grandmother told them to me. She learned the stories from her grandfather, and so on, back many, many years throughout time."

"Tell them the one about how the squirrel taught the elephant some manners," suggested Grandma.

"Many years ago, in Africa, a squirrel got in the way of an elephant walking down a path. The mighty elephant knocked the little squirrel aside. The squirrel was rather annoyed with the elephant and said, 'You think you are so mighty, Elephant. I may be very small, but I bet that I can eat ten times as much as you!'

"The elephant roared with laughter. 'I know I am the most magnificent animal in the jungle,' he said. 'How could a puny creature such as yourself eat even *one-tenth* of what I can eat? I shall put you in your place,' gloated the elephant.

"So, the animals gathered huge piles of nuts for the squirrel and the elephant. They decided that the contest would begin the next morning.

"The next day, the squirrel and elephant took their places at the nut piles and began to eat. Confidently, Elephant munched away. He was sure that he'd win. Squirrel nibbled quickly and was soon full. In fact, he was so full that he thought he would burst. He glanced over at Elephant who paid him no mind. Quietly, Squirrel scampered away as his brother, who was hiding in the bush, slipped quickly back to Squirrel's nut pile. The brother ate away until he was full also, and then he, too, slipped away, sending in another relative to take his place. This went on all day.

"After a while, Elephant noticed that Squirrel was still eating. 'Had enough?' he asked.

" 'Not yet, Elephant,' replied Squirrel.

"By nightfall, Elephant could not eat another nut. He looked at Squirrel and raised his trunk. 'Squirrel, you win,' he said. Squirrel, who had slipped back to the nut pile at the end of the day, hopped up and down, clapping. From that day on, Elephant was kinder to Squirrel and gave him the respect he deserved."

"Well, it seems like the squirrel had a lot more brains than that silly ostrich," laughed Jamal.

"Many folktales use animals to tell stories that have a meaning or a moral to them," explained Grandpa.

"Please tell us another story, Grandpa," insisted Kira.

"Well, it looks like we'll be in the dark for some time," observed Grandpa. "Have I ever told you the story about how the sun got into the sky?"

11

"A long time ago, the sun lived here on Earth at the base of a very high mountain. The sun and the sea were good friends. The sun would visit the sea, and they would grill burgers and have a good time together."

"Oh, Grandpa, they didn't really grill hamburgers, did they?" asked Kira as Jamal rolled his eyes.

"Well, no, I just threw that in there because that's what makes telling tales so much fun," Grandpa chuckled. "Anyway, the sun would get sad because the sea never came to visit. The sea answered, 'I fear I might drown you, Sun, for your house is not big enough to hold back my waters.'

" 'Then I shall build you a pool for your waters,' replied the sun.

"When the pool was finished, the sea agreed to visit the sun, and soon the sea's waters began to fill the pool.

"The sea kept coming, and the waters began to overflow the sides of the pool. The sun, being very proud, did not tell the sea to stop. Soon the waters began to flow up the sides of the mountain. Up and up rose the waters, until the sun stood at the very top of the mountain. At last, the waters of the sea covered the mountaintop, and with no place left to go, the sun leapt into the sky. After a time, the sea went back to its home, but the sun never came back to the mountain and has stayed high up in the sky ever since."

"That's a lovely story," said Kira.

"Many folktales are told to explain things in nature. Some folktales explain how Earth came to be. Others tell how the stars got into the sky, and still others tell how mountains, rivers, and lakes were created."

Jamal realized that he hadn't thought once about watching television or playing video games.

"Someday, I will tell my grandchildren these same stories!" Kira said as Grandpa and Grandma exchanged smiles.

Now the thunder and lightning were fading into the night, but the rain still fell gently. Far off in the distance, it looked as if the moon was trying to peek through the dark clouds.

"Please, Grandpa, tell us another," begged Kira.

"Well," said Grandpa, who didn't need to be asked twice, "have I told you the story about how the moon. . . ."

Think Critically

1. How do Jamal's feelings about folktales change during the story?

2. What does Elephant learn in the story of Elephant and Squirrel?

3. Why do you think Grandpa likes telling stories?

4. How do the folktales in the story differ? How are they alike?

5. Of the folktales that Grandpa told, which was your favorite? Explain.

 Social Studies

Traditional Tales Look up some traditional folktales from other countries. Make a list of tales, the countries they come from, and what they explain. Find each country on a globe.

School-Home Connection Ask members of your family whether they know of any folktales they can share with you. Then tell family members one of the folktales in this book.